HUXLEY
IN THE HAUNTED HOUSE

RODNEY PEPPÉ

FANTAIL

Huxley Pig snuggled down underneath his big, cosy bedcover, took a sip of his bedtime cocoa and opened the strange old book his Granny had given him.

"Crumbs!," said Huxley to himself. "There are some pretty creepy stories in this book. It's all about ghosts and ghouls and things that go bump in the night!"

Huxley started to read and the more he read, the more creepy the book became until he was almost too frightened to turn another page. Just then there was a RUSTLE-RUSTLE sort of noise from the curtains. Huxley wasn't sure if a RUSTLE-RUSTLE sort of noise really counted as a thing that goes bump in the night, but he wasn't taking any chances.

"Is-is that you, Sam?" Huxley whispered, desperately hoping that it was his friend, Sam Seagull, at the window and not a ghost or ghoul.

"Squark!" said Sam, poking his head through the curtains.

"Thank goodness!" gasped Huxley. "Come over here beside me."

"This is a really spooky book, Sam," said Huxley. "There certainly aren't many jokes here. Look at that – a blank page. Must be a picture of a ghost in a snowstorm! Ha-ha!"

"Squark!" said Sam, flipping the page with his beak before Huxley could think of any more awful jokes.

"Let's read the first story," Huxley suggested. "It's called "The Haunted House" and this is how it starts . . . 'It was a misty, moonless night as the shadowy figure crept stealthily . . .' Er . . . m-maybe we should look at the p-pictures first, Sam."

Huxley wasn't exactly what you might call an utterly fearless pig.

"Squark!" said Sam (not an utterly fearless seagull) glancing round to make sure that no shadowy figures were stealthily creeping up on them.

"Here's a picture of the haunted house," said Huxley. "I wonder what it would be like to live there?"

And with that Huxley drifted off into a dream about haunted houses, ghosts, ghouls and things that go bump in the night . . .

The heavy wooden door creaked slowly open and Huxley and Sam timidly entered the gloomy hallway.

"A-are you there?" called Huxley.

" 'Course I am!" squawked Sam.

"No, not you!" Huxley frowned. "I meant the agent from 'Holiday Haunts' who wants to rent us this place."

"Well . . . is that 'im?" asked Sam, pointing.

"Who? Oh, Sam!" said Huxley. "That's just a suit of armour. You often find them in old houses. Come on, let's look around."

Huxley walked on into the main hall and Sam went to follow but just as he stepped forward, he was certain he saw the suit of armour move its head – as though it were watching him!

" 'Ere, 'Uxley!" shrieked Sam. "That pile of old tin cans just moved!"

"Nonsense, Sam," scolded Huxley. "You're just imagining things."

"This place gives me the creeps," muttered Sam.

"You just don't appreciate fine old buildings," said Huxley.

"Is this 'im, then?" asked Sam.

"No, Sam," sighed Huxley. "This is just a portrait."

"Of a vampire," added Sam.

"Well," said Huxley, "I will admit that he's a bit long in the tooth! Ha-ha! Now, where did I put that 'Holiday Haunts' brochure?"

Huxley rummaged in his big red lunch box and pulled out a cheese sandwich along with the 'Holiday Haunts' brochure.

"It shays ig here . . ." spluttered Huxley, spraying bits of bread and cheddar everywhere, "that we should . . ."

" 'Ere, 'Uxley," interrupted Sam. "That geezer just winked at me!"

"What ARE you talking about?" said Huxley, flicking crumbs off the brochure. "What 'geezer'?"

"Old Dracula up there," answered Sam, "just winked at me!"

"I think you must be going potty, Sam," said Huxley. "That's only a portrait, you know."

Sam sighed and looked up at the painting. Sure enough, slowly and deliberately, the vampire smiled and winked one eye. Sam gulped and hurried over beside Huxley.

At that moment the big wooden door creaked open and a red and white spotted tie rushed in closely followed by a rather breathless rodent.

"Hello," he gasped. "I'm your 'Holiday Haunts' agent. I'm sorry I'm late but the traffic in Transylvania is terrible these days . . . why, it's Huxley Pig!"

"Horace!" cried Huxley. "Fancy meeting you here!"

"Have you had a chance to look round this charming residence?" asked Horace.

"Not really," Huxley replied, "but it looks very nice."

"Nice?" said Horace, a little taken aback. "You mean you like it?"

"Of course," Huxley assured him, "although Sam here thinks it's haunted."

"Haunted?!" squeaked Horace nervously. "Oh, dear me, no! Ha-ha! Haunted? Certainly not! It is er . . . full of character, though. Look at this beautiful solid wood panelling."

Horace knocked three times on a wooden panel to show how robust it was and was immediately answered by an eerie KNOCK! KNOCK! KNOCK! from the panel!

"Er . . . must be an echo," he hastily explained.

Suddenly, the mysterious panel spun round and a tall figure in a dark suit appeared.

"Vile Vincent at your service, gentlemen," said the stranger in a voice so deep and sinister that Huxley had to sit down and eat three chocolate biscuits from his lunch box to calm his nerves.

"How did you get in here?" asked Horace.

"I expect he had a skeleton key! Ha-ha!" joked Huxley, feeling better after a spot of biscuit therapy.

"Precisely so, sir," hissed Vile Vincent glaring straight at Huxley in such a flesh-creepingly, hair-tinglingly frightening way that Huxley was forced to have another biscuit.

"This is your butler, Huxley," said Horace. "To call him, just ring this little bell."

Horace produced a hand bell and tinkled it quietly. All at once an enormous roar thundered through the house. It was a roar so loud that it made Huxley's teeth chatter and rattled the lid of his lunch box.

"Wh-what was that roar?" stammered Huxley, reaching for another biscuit.

"Roar? What roar?" said Horace, obviously pretending he hadn't heard it. "Did you hear anything, Vincent?"

"A slight rumble, sir," replied Vile Vincent. "Cuddles thought that was his dinner bell."

"Cuddles . . . who is Cuddles?" asked Huxley.

"Oh, er, just the household pet," smiled Horace. "He comes with the place . . . like Vincent."

" 'Ere, is this Cuddles' collar?" squawked Sam, waddling in with a massive studded collar around his waist. " 'E must be a pretty big dog! Ha-ha!"

"Well, yes and no, sir," said Vile Vincent, taking the collar from Sam.

"What do you mean?" Huxley asked.

"Yes, he is pretty big – and no, he's not a dog," said Vincent, then he disappeared through the secret panel.

"What sort of pet is this then, Horace?" demanded Huxley. "It's not a dog and it certainly doesn't sound like a budgie, so what is it?"

"You are about to find out," said Horace gravely.

They could hear Cuddles coming before they saw him. His footsteps shook the floor like mini earthquakes and he puffed and panted like an old steam train.

"Down, Cuddles! Down boy!" they could hear Vile Vincent scream.

"I'd better warn you," whispered Horace. "Cuddles likes to play games and they can get . . . er . . . a bit lively!"

"I don't like the sound of this, 'Uxley," grumbled Sam. "Let's go 'ome."

At that moment, Cuddles burst into the room, dragging Vile Vincent behind him. Cuddles looked absolutely huge to Huxley and Sam, but that's probably because he WAS absolutely huge -- and green and ferocious and terrifying too!

"Sit, Cuddles!" screamed Vile Vincent, "remember your pet training!"

"Oh, all right," said Cuddles. "I was only having a little fun. You know how much I like to eat . . . er . . . MEET new people. Hello everyone!"

Cuddles sat down with a tremendous thump that raised little puffs of dust from between the floorboards.

Huxley wasn't quite sure how to deal with an absolutely huge, green, ferocious, terrifying monster so he talked about his favourite subject instead – food.

"It says in the brochure that all meals are provided," he pointed out. "Well, I'm starving!"

"Ah, yes," said Horace. "I'm afraid the cook left in rather a hurry and . . ."

"Cuddles will do the cooking," announced Vile Vincent. "Won't you Cuddles?"

"Love to!" said Cuddles, smiling sweetly – or as sweetly as an absolutely huge, green, ferocious, terrifying monster can smile. "I'm a brilliant cook. I'll make you all scrumptious monster burgers!"

Horace, Sam and Huxley set the table while Cuddles and Vile Vincent busied themselves in the kitchen.

"Well, will you rent the house?" asked Horace once they had sat down.

"That all really depends on Cuddles' cooking," said Huxley just as Vile Vincent appeared with their meal.

"You'll just adore this!" called Cuddles, peering over Vincent's shoulder.

"Your monster burgers, gentlemen," said Vile Vincent, placing in front of each of them a plate piled high with the biggest and most curious mountain of bun and burger that Huxley had ever seen.

"There's certainly plenty of it," Huxley said, clearly impressed by the sheer size.

"Go on, take a bite!" said Cuddles. "You'll love it. It's my favourite." Huxley opened his mouth as wide as he could – wider than he could ever remember opening it before, in fact – and sank his teeth into the monster burger.

"This," drooled Huxley, "is going to be just . . . BLEEUGH!!" Huxley spat the mouthful of monster burger out onto his plate even though he knew that polite pigs never do such things. It tasted utterly revolting.

"You don't like it, do you?" sighed Cuddles. "I can tell."

"What on earth did you put in it?" asked Huxley.

"Just the usual things," said Cuddles. "Slugs, earwigs, caterpillars, beetles, worms . . . no, I tell a lie, it was wood lice, not worms."

"And then there was a toad," continued Cuddles, "a little mud and some green slime sauce. No salt, additives or artificial colouring."

"Well, that does it, Horace," said Huxley. "I could get used to monsters, vampires, spooks' portraits and moving armour, but I can't rent the place if the food is going to be this bad."

"Shhh!" hissed Horace at Huxley, seeing how dejected Cuddles looked. "You've upset Cuddles now!"

"Perhaps if you offered to play a little game, he might perk up again," suggested Vile Vincent.

"Would he?" said Huxley. He hadn't really wanted to hurt Cuddles' feelings. "Would you like to play a game, Cuddles?"

"Oooh, yes, please!" cooed Cuddles.

"What's your favourite game?" Huxley asked.

"Swallow my leader!" replied Cuddles.

"I think you mean follow my leader," Huxley corrected.

"I know what I mean!" roared Cuddles, lunging towards the table. Huxley, Sam and Horace leapt to their feet and Cuddles chased them round the furniture. Round and round and round and round . . .

Huxley felt his legs were still running when he woke up safely snuggled down under his big, cosy bedcover.

"My goodness, what a dream!" he said to Sam, who was still perched on his bed.

"Squark?" said Sam, a little confused.

"Well, I dreamt a monster was chasing us round and round . . ." said Huxley. "Oh, dear I feel a little giddy. I think I'll have a glass of water."

Huxley got up only to plonk his foot down on something squidgy which made a strange SQUELCH-SLURP noise.

"Look at this, Sam!" he cried. "It's a monster burger! Well, well, maybe it wasn't all just a dream after all. I'm glad Cuddles wasn't too good at playing swallow my leader, though! Ha-ha! Fancy some slightly squashed slugs, earwigs, caterpillars, beetles . . ."